Ronald McDonald

and the Tale of
the Talking Plant

By John Albano
Illustrated by John Costanza

A GOLDEN BOOK • NEW YORK

Western Publishing Company, Inc., Racine, Wisconsin 53404

RONALD McDONALD and the Grimace often took
walks through the deep forest.

"Look!" said Ronald during one of their walks. "The
flowers are in bloom!"

"The flowers are very pretty," said the Grimace. Then he heard a noise. "I think I hear the weeping willows weeping, Ronald!"

"Weeping willows don't weep," said Ronald.

Suddenly Ronald saw who was really crying—two children sitting in the bushes. "It's Roy and Joy!" he shouted.

"YOW!" cried the Grimace, who was so startled by the shout that he flipped several feet into the air.

The children felt better when they saw
Ronald and the Grimace. They had all been
friends for a long time.

"I'll bet you two are crying because you're
lost," said Ronald.

"That's right," answered Roy. "But there's
more to it than that."

Roy explained that he and Joy had gotten lost in the forest while playing a game of hide-and-seek.

Then Joy told Ronald and the Grimace that a plant in the forest had talked to them!

"We asked the talking plant if it knew the way out of the forest," said Joy.

"It said that it knew the way," added Roy. "But it wouldn't tell us. We got scared, and ran away!"

"Plants are usually very nice," said Ronald. "I can't understand this!"

Ronald promised to show the children the way out of the forest. "But first," he said, "I want to find that plant, and ask it why it wouldn't help you."

They all set out to search for the talking plant.

Before long, they came to a wide, muddy river. The Grimace walked into the river and began to make his way across. "We can *wade* across," he said confidently. "The mud probably isn't deep!"

The Grimace was wrong. With each step, he sank deeper and deeper into the mud. Before long, he was stuck.

"Duh, Ronald, I think I'm stuck!" the embarrassed Grimace called back.

Ronald reached into his pocket, and using magic,
he pulled out something made of wood. It was a bridge,
all rolled up into a bundle!

Roy and Joy were astounded.

"How did Ronald do that?" asked Roy.

Joy just smiled and said, "Ronald can do anything!"

Ronald placed the bridge on the ground and waved his hand. SWOOSH! The bridge unrolled and sprang straight across the mud river. It then fastened itself to the other side.

Ronald walked to the middle of the bridge, and pulled the Grimace to safety.

"There now," said Ronald. "This is a much easier way to cross the river!"

They all walked across the bridge and continued searching the forest.

The search went on for a long time. Just when it seemed they would never find the talking plant, a strange voice called from behind the trees.

"Come over here, please," it begged.

"YOW!" screamed the Grimace, who was so startled by the voice that he flipped over once again.

They all rushed toward the voice. There, behind some trees, was the talking plant.

Spreading its delicate flowers, the plant cooed, "Come closer and look at me. Am I not beautiful?"

"You are pretty," answered Ronald. "But why wouldn't you help these children?"

"There is never anyone around when my beautiful flowers come into bloom," the plant explained. "When I saw children in the forest, I did not want them to leave. I only wanted someone to see my flowers. I never meant to frighten the children!"

Joy felt sorry for the plant. "Can you help the talking plant?" she asked Ronald.

Once again, Ronald reached into his pocket. This time he pulled out a clear globe.

He tossed it into the air, and—POOF!—it burst into tiny sparks.

The tiny sparks floated down onto the plant and—PRESTO—the plant vanished!

Ronald led his friends out of the forest and guided them to the town square. There, in the center of a garden, was the talking plant!

"This is the plant's new home," said Ronald. "Now many people will come every day to see and enjoy its beauty."

The talking plant was so delighted, it invited each
of its four friends to pick a flower.

"Thanks to all of you," the plant said. "Please come
back and visit soon!"

Roy and Joy thanked
Ronald and the Grimace
for all their help. Then
they waved good bye and
left for home.

Ronald was puzzled
when he saw that the
Grimace didn't have the
flower he had picked.
"Where's your flower?"
Ronald asked.

The Grimace puffed up his chest proudly. "I put it on that young tree," he said, "so people will notice *it*, too!"

"Why, Grimace," said Ronald playfully, "you're a regular gardener!"